IMAGINE THAT

Licensed exclusively to Imagine That Publishing Ltd
Tide Mill Way, Woodbridge, Suffolk, IP12 1AP, UK
www.imaginethat.com
Copyright © 2017 Imagine That Group Ltd
All rights reserved
2 4 6 8 9 7 5 3
Manufactured in China

Retold by Stephanie Dragone
Illustrated by Jennie Poh

ISBN 978-1-78700-183-1

A catalogue record for this book is available from the British Library

For three much-loved and special
children, Jannah, Myles and Archer.

Pinocchio

Retold by Stephanie Dragone

Illustrated by Jennie Poh

Once upon a time, there was a lonely old man called Geppetto who had no children. Geppetto wished that he had a son to love and keep him company, so he carved himself a puppet that looked just like a little boy.

He called his puppet Pinocchio.

But things didn't go quite as planned. Pinocchio didn't want to stay at home with Geppetto. All he wanted was to have fun and adventures, so he ran away!

After some time, naughty Pinocchio came home. He felt sorry for running away and he was very pleased to see Geppetto again.

As Pinocchio ate the food that Geppetto had lovingly prepared for him, he heard a tiny voice. There, on his arm, sat a cricket ... and it was talking!

'Pinocchio! You must be good,' said the cricket, 'or every time you tell a lie or do something bad, your nose will grow.'

For a little while, Pinocchio was happy to be home again. He promised Geppetto that he would be good, and that he would go to school every day.

SCHOOL

Geppetto was very poor,
so he had to sell his coat to buy
Pinocchio an ABC book for school,
but he didn't mind. He loved Pinocchio.

The next day, Pinocchio was on his way to school when he heard music. In the middle of the village square stood a puppet theatre.

'If only I could see the puppet show,' sighed Pinocchio. 'But I don't have any money.'

Then he had a brilliant idea. 'I know,' he cried, 'I'll sell my ABC book!' So he did, and his nose started to grow!

Book Shop

A B C

Pinocchio queued up to buy a ticket for the puppet show. While he was waiting, a fox and a cat came up to him.

'Good morning,' said the fox slyly, looking at the coins in Pinocchio's hand. 'I see you only have enough money for one show.'

Then, coming closer, he whispered, 'I can take you to a magic field where you can plant your money and make it grow!'

Pinocchio really liked this idea. If he grew more money, he could buy another ABC book and go to as many puppet shows as he liked, so he set off with the fox and the cat.

Soon, they stopped for a rest. As the sleepy fox and cat began to snore loudly, the cricket suddenly appeared again.

'Don't trust them,' he whispered in Pinocchio's ear. But Pinocchio took no notice, and when the fox and the cat woke up they all set off again.

After a long journey, they arrived at the magic field, and Pinocchio planted his coins. While he was waiting for them to grow, he had a little nap, but when he woke up all he saw was an empty hole! The fox and the cat had tricked him and stolen his money!

'Don't worry,' said a sweet voice. Looking up,
Pinocchio saw a blue fairy fluttering close by.
'I can explain everything to Geppetto,' she
said kindly, 'but you must promise to be good.'

'I promise!' cried Pinocchio happily.

After being tricked by the fox and the cat, Pinocchio behaved himself for a long time. Then one day, on his way to school, he passed a group of children. 'Come with us!' they cried.

Forgetting his promise to be good,
Pinocchio followed them to a place
where children play all day long.

Pinocchio had great fun playing
with the children until, one night,
the cricket appeared again.

'Pinocchio! If you don't go home
you'll turn into a donkey,'
he said, very seriously.

This time, Pinocchio listened to the cricket. He ran and ran until he arrived at the sea. He was wondering what to do next when a seagull flew overhead.

'You must help Geppetto!' cried the seagull.
'He set off in a boat to find you and a huge
fish swallowed him!'

And with that, Pinocchio leapt into the sea and
started swimming. He had to save Geppetto!

Suddenly, an enormous fish appeared out of the water ... and swallowed Pinocchio in one giant gulp!

Inside the fish's tummy, Pinocchio heard
a sound ... a voice he knew and loved.
It was Geppetto!

That night, while the great fish slept, Pinocchio
and Geppetto crawled out of its enormous mouth
and swam safely to shore. Then they made
their way home, together.

From that day on, Pinocchio went to school every day, and he was always good.

One day, the blue fairy came to visit.

'I think it's time to reward both of you,' she said. And with that, she turned Pinocchio into a real little boy!

At long last, Geppetto had the son he had always wished for.